Dedicated with much love to Dave,
    — you have nourished this book in so many ways, thank you,
and to Juan Pablito,
    — may you always be touched by the beauty of the world.

The idea for this book was inspired by my experience volunteering with the school tours program at the Vancouver Art Gallery. The images in this book were inspired by prominent Canadian artists and are based specifically on the work of the following painters (in order of appearance): Emily Carr, E.J. Hughes, Lawren Harris, Ivan Eyre, William Kurelek, Tom Thomson, J.E.H. MacDonald, Clarence A. Gagnon, J. P. Lemieux, Alex Colville, Christopher Pratt and David Blackwood.

For more information please visit the book's website:
www.picturescape.ca

Special thanks to David Cross, Dimiter Savoff, Doug McCaffry, Tiffany Stone, Jesse Finkelstein, Stacey Noyes, James Baker, Suzanne Cross, Marcel and Angela Morin, Gillian Hunt and Lincoln Heller for their gracious help and support.

First published in 2005
by Simply Read Books Inc
www.simplyreadbooks.com

© 2005 Elisa Gutiérrez

STORY CONTRIBUTIONS BY TIFFANY STONE AND DAVID CROSS
BOOK DESIGN BY ELISA GUTIÉRREZ
PHOTOGRAPHY AND IMAGING BY SCANLAB

LIBRARY AND ARCHIVES CANADA CATALOGUING IN PUBLICATION

Gutiérrez, Elisa, 1972-
  Picturescape / Elisa Gutiérrez.

ISBN 1-894965-24-8

  1. Art, Canadian--Juvenile fiction. 2. Art museums--Canada--Juvenile fiction. 3. Canada--Description and travel--Juvenile fiction. Stories without words. I Title.

PS8613.U88P52 2005   jC813'.6   C2005-900579-3

Printed in China

10 9 8 7 6 5 4 3 2 1

picturescape

Elisa Gutiérrez

SIMPLY READ BOOKS

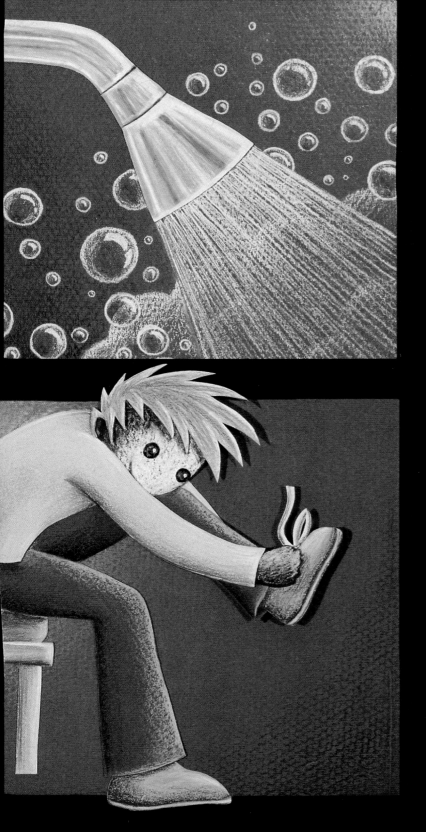

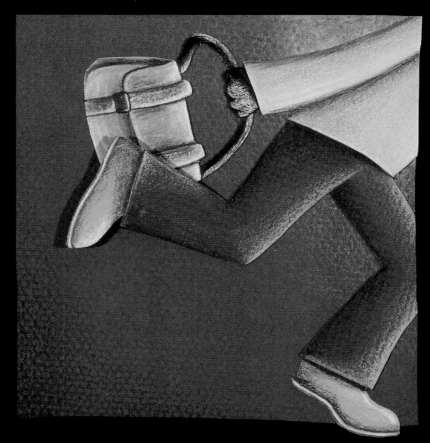

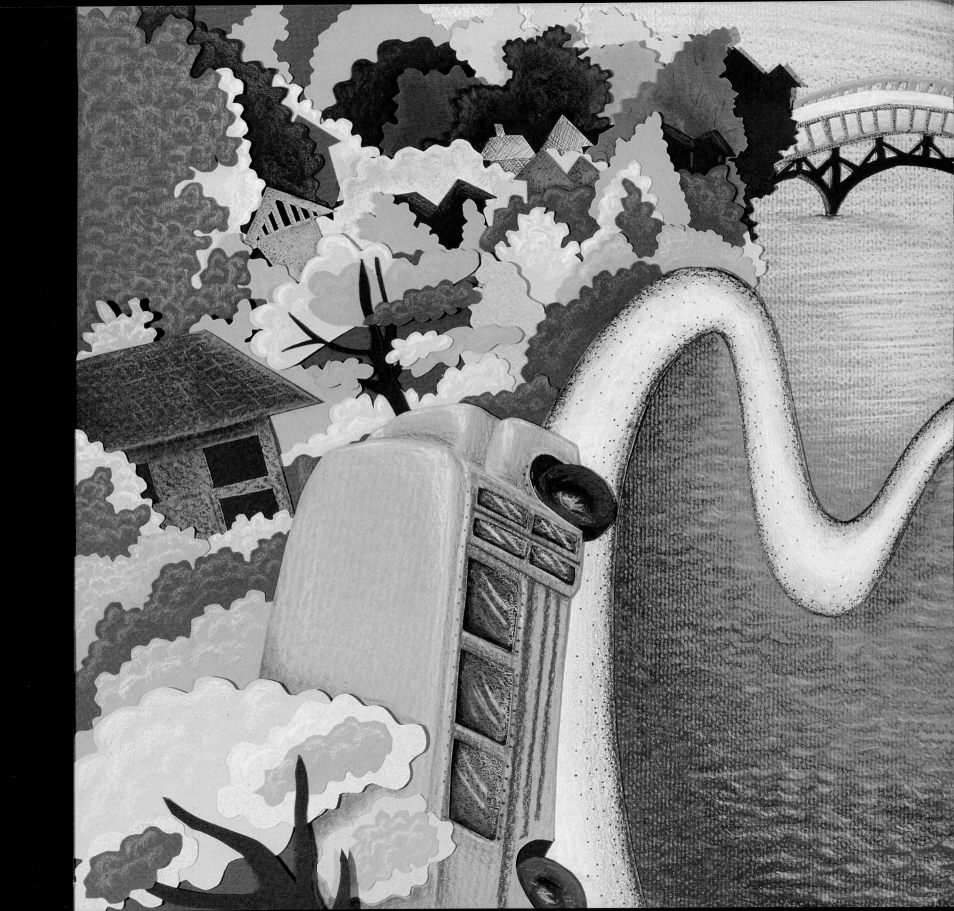

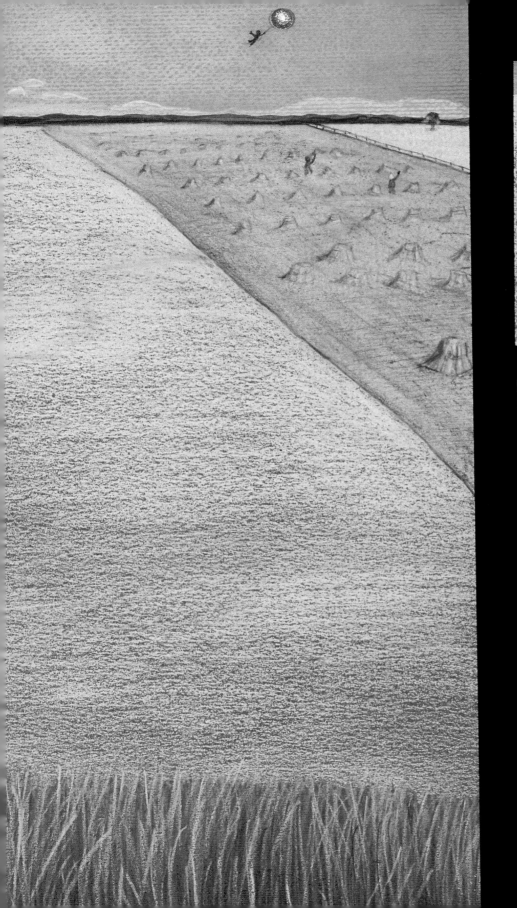

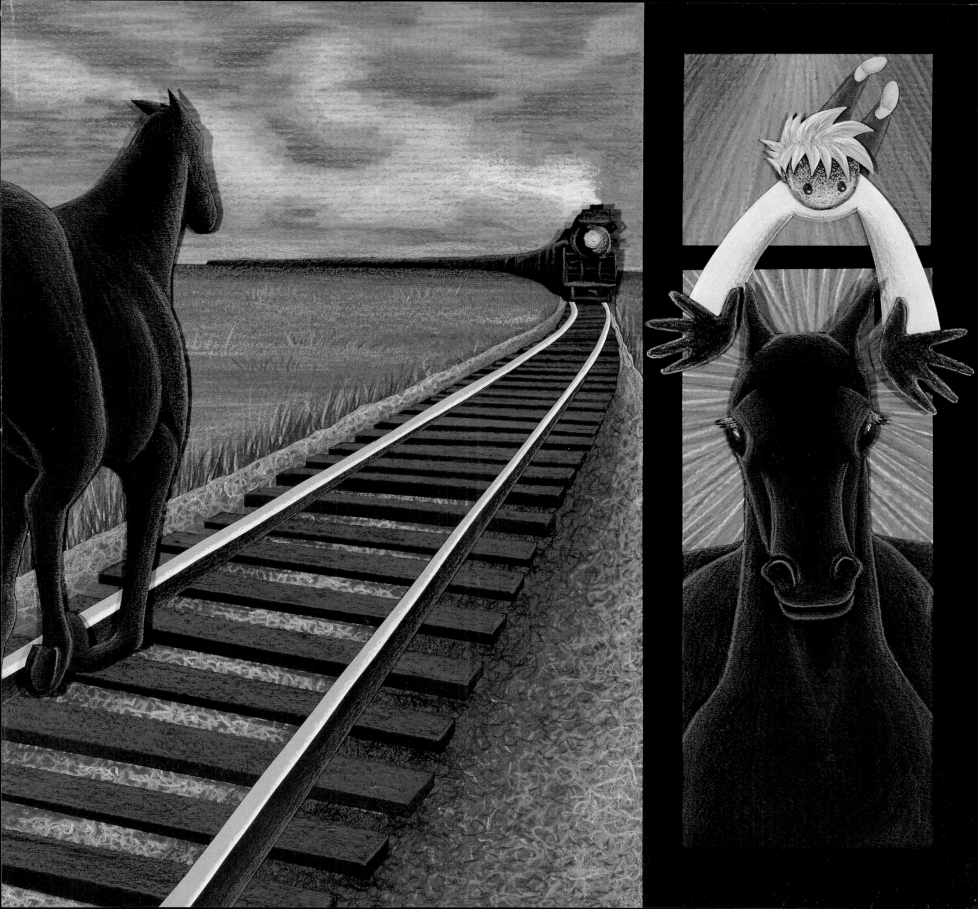

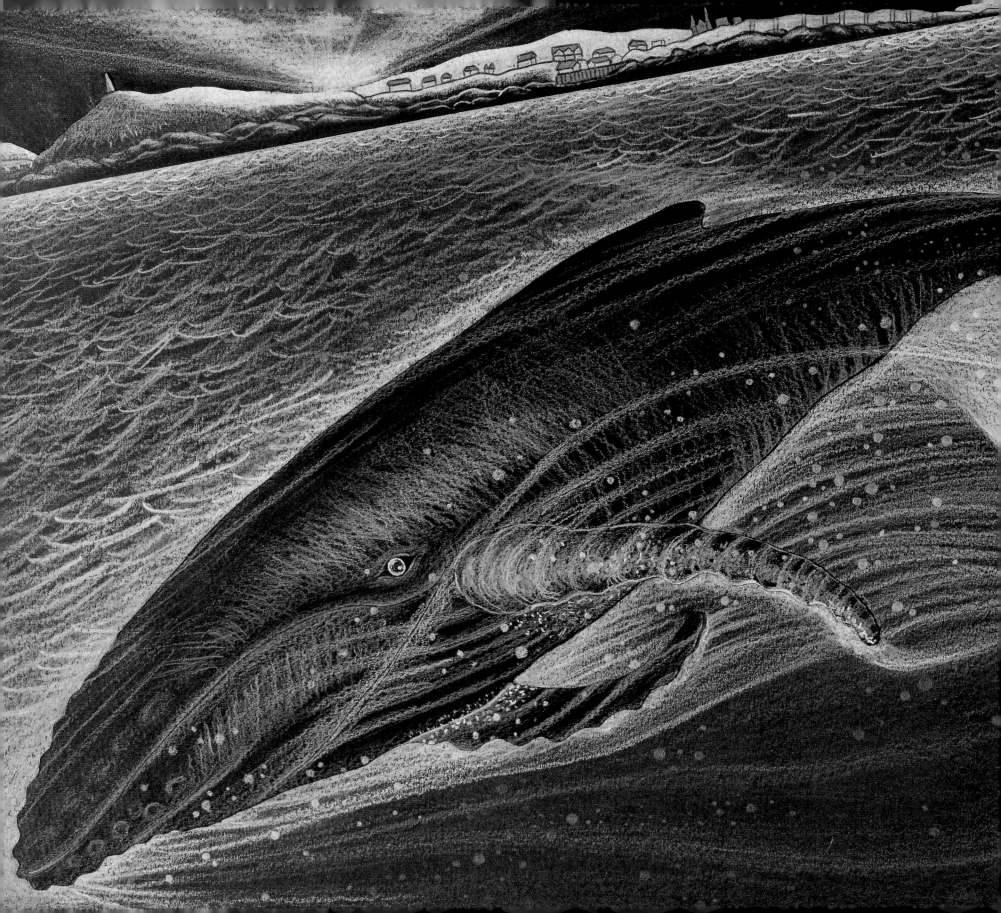

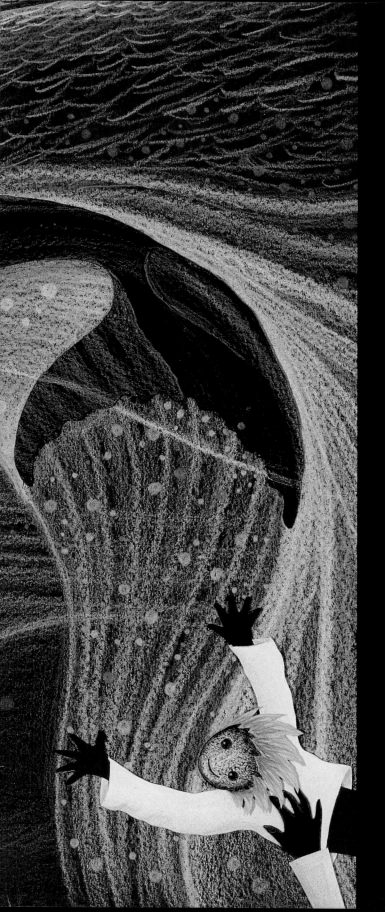

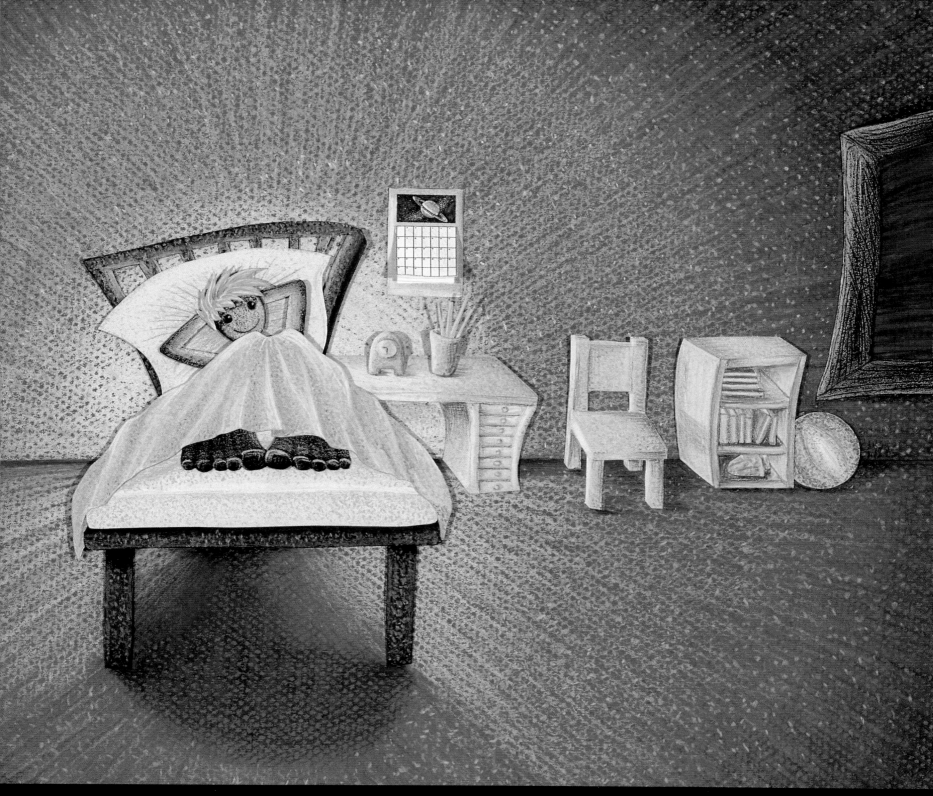